Cocaine
The Rush to Destruction

ILLICIT AND MISUSED DRUGS

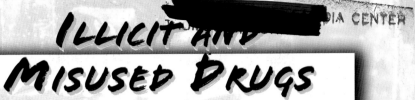

ILLICIT AND MISUSED DRUGS

Cocaine
The Rush to Destruction

by Zachary Chastain

Mason Crest Publishers
Philadelphia

Mason Crest Publishers Inc.
370 Reed Road
Broomall, Pennsylvania 19008
(866) MCP-BOOK (toll free)
www.masoncrest.com

First printing
1 2 3 4 5 6 7 8 9 10
Library of Congress Cataloging-in-Publication Data
ISBN-13: 978-1-4222-0149-7 (series)

Chastain, Zachary.
  Cocaine : the rush to destruction / by Zachary Chastain.
      p. cm. — (Illicit and misused drugs)
  Includes bibliographical references and index.
  ISBN-13: 978-1-4222-0154-1
  1. Cocaine—Juvenile literature. 2. Cocaine abuse—Juvenile lit-
erature. I. Title. II. Series.

  HV5810.C53 2008
  613.8'4—dc22

                                          2006029212

Interior design by Benjamin Stewart.
Cover design by MK Bassett-Harvey.
Produced by Harding House Publishing Service Inc.
Vestal, New York.
www.hardinghousepages.com

Cover image design by Peter Spires Culotta.
Cover photography: iStock Photography (Tomaz Levstek)
Printed in the Hashemite Kingdom of Jordan.

This book is meant to educate and should not be used as an alternative to appropriate medical care. Its creators have made every effort to ensure that the
information presented is accurate—but it is not intended to substitute for the
help and services of trained professionals.

 # CONTENTS

INTRODUCTION

Addicting drugs are among the greatest challenges to health, well-being, and the sense of independence and freedom for which we all strive—and yet these drugs are present in the everyday lives of most people. Almost every home has alcohol or tobacco waiting to be used, and has medicine cabinets stocked with possibly outdated but still potentially deadly drugs. Almost everyone has a friend or loved one with an addiction-related problem. Almost everyone seems to have a solution neatly summarized by word or phrase: medicalization, legalization, criminalization, war-on-drugs.

For better and for worse, drug information seems to be everywhere, but what information sources can you trust? How do you separate misinformation (whether deliberate or born of ignorance and prejudice) from the facts? Are prescription drugs safer than "street" drugs? Is occasional drug use really harmful? Is cigarette smoking more addictive than heroin? Is marijuana safer than alcohol? Are the harms caused by drug use limited to the users? Can some people become addicted following just a few exposures? Is treatment or counseling just for those with serious addiction problems?

These are just a few of the many questions addressed in this series. It is an empowering series because it provides the information and perspectives that can help people come to their own opinions and find answers to the challenges posed by drugs in their own lives. The series also provides further resources for information and assistance, recognizing that no single source has all the answers. It should be of interest and relevance to areas of study spanning biology, chemistry, history, health, social studies and more. Its efforts to provide a real-world context for the information that is clearly presented but not overly simplified should be appreciated by students, teachers, and parents.

The series is especially commendable in that it does not pretend to pose easy answers or imply that all decisions can be made on the basis of simple facts: some challenges have no immediate or simple solutions, and some solutions will need to rely as much upon basic values as basic facts. Despite this, the series should help to at least provide a foundation of knowledge. In the end, it may help as much by pointing out where the solutions are not simple, obvious, or known to work. In fact, at many points, the reader is challenged to think for him- or herself by being asked what his or her opinion is.

A core concept of the series is to recognize that we will never have all the facts, and many of the decisions will never be easy. Hopefully, however, armed with information, perspective, and resources, readers will be better prepared for taking on the challenges posed by addictive drugs in everyday life.

— *Jack E. Henningfield, Ph.D.*

1 What Is Cocaine?

Imagine a mountain pass deep in the ancient kingdom of the Inca. Silhouetted against the dawn, a **Quechua** man drives a herd of llamas bearing bundles of leaves on their backs. The man is chewing as he runs.

When he and the animals reach a vast plateau, they stop at a circle of stones, set by the man's people to mark the paths of the sun and the stars. As the sun's first shafts of light strike the stones, the man turns clockwise from the east to face each of the four directions. Then he raises his voice in song and casts handfuls of leaves from the llamas back into the wind. The leaves scatter over the land. Once again, the man faces east, his eyes fixed on the sun. He stretches himself out flat in an act of prayer and adoration to the sun god.

A coca plant is seen here in full bloom. Only the leaves are harvested for human consumption.

As the sun's rays climb higher on the stones, the man gets slowly to his feet. He takes more leaves from the llamas' backs and then squats to prepare more leaves for his next chew. From a tiny gourd that hangs from his belt, he adds to the leaves a dash of gray ash-lime. He has now made ready for another *cocada*, the unit of distance that measures his world—the distance he can run before he needs to prepare another cocada. He puts the leaves in his mouth, begins to chew, and slaps the rump of the lead llama. His mind clear, his muscles strong, the man is ready to continue his journey.

Now consider this first-person story from www.interdope. com/cocexp7.html:

> For the past six months [a new drug] has entered my life. I have tried a variety of drugs, I have found that stimulants are what I like. . . . It wasn't until my sophomore year of college that I ever even thought of trying [this drug]. It was just something that I looked at as such a "hard drug," something that only people that were really into drugs tried. While at school I moved into a new apartment and soon found my roommate selling a little. When she first started doing that I found myself with very easy access to the drug.
>
> At first I found the effects when I went out and drank a little, danced, and did a few bumps to be almost similar to the rolling ecstasy feeling. Since then this has become an every weekend event for me. In a way it almost scares me. I don't feel like I have a problem. I work very hard in school, get good grades . . . but when it comes to the weekends I feel like I can party hard too. Since this

has started for me I have experienced many nights that seem like a movie. Not quite similar to *Human Traffic* or *Go* or anything of that nature. But, there have been times when I have woken up and been like "I had a really good time last night but what . . . happened?" I have lost my keys at a bar doing bumps in the bathroom and then leaving my keys on the toilet seat. I have slept with someone that I would have never considered sleeping with. And I have also told a best guy friend of mine my true feelings for him, that I never had the courage to say before. I have ups and downs with the drug.

Lately, it has been conflicting with school. I have been doing it on school nights which sucks cause I have an 8 o'clock class. But, many times it has helped me stay up and actually has helped me get work done. But, each time there is a certain feeling of preoccupation that I just cannot escape. . . . There are some things that I have said and done because of cocaine that I wish I could take back, but really I am just in awe of the drug right now. I have never found something that has allowed me to be myself as much as this has. However, there is a downside whenever I find myself trying to go to bed, I cannot stand that restless feeling that I have. . . . Lately before I try and go to sleep I have been taking this prescription cold medicine called Guaifenex which adds a hallucinogenic state to the drug's come-down.

I don't know how to express my feeling with this drug. The only thing I can say and mean is that it is the only drug I have ever tried that has me thinking about it all the time. I cannot afford

A person who snorts cocaine may experience positive "benefits" from the drug, but at the same time he is likely to find that his drug use conflicts with his ability to carry on the activities of daily life.

Bogota is the capital city of Colombia, the nation that produces 80 percent of the world's cocaine.

14   Chapter 1—What Is Cocaine?

to do it all the times that I think about it but. . . Many times I have laid in bed alone on the come-down and questioned my actions of that night, and regretted nearly all of them. And as many times as I have said I am never doing this again I always find myself looking for a bag. I do not have any advice for others except use in moderation, which is how I try to use everything. I don't like being out of control.

What do these two individuals, separated by thousands of miles and hundreds of years, have in common? Both are experiencing the effects of a chemical found in the plant *Erythroxylum coca*, native to South America. When you add the suffix that stands for alkaloid chemicals to the name of the coca plant, you get—cocaine.

An Ancient Plant

For centuries, the coca leaf has been chewed by South American natives, and in some parts of South America, coca remains an important part of the culture. Coca has seen varied and regular use

Coca and Spirituality

The Indians of South America use coca leaves for divination of the spirit world. The veins of coca leaves are said to be pathways through the mysteries of the ancient past as well as the mysteries of our own age. It is even said that the Virgin Mary chewed on the coca as she mourned the loss of her son, leaving her teeth marks on the back of the leaves. Quechua shaman may use coca to cross "the bridge of smoke," entering the world of spirits and activating their magical powers.

throughout its history. It was originally a sacred plant, reserved for Incan royalty, but has evolved into the contemporary plant we know today—cultivated for the powerful drug in its leaves and distributed to many classes of people with many different intentions. Today, cocaine is known mostly for its abuse. It is one of the world's most powerful stimulants of natural origin.

Coca is thought to be specifically native to the eastern slopes of the Andes. Nature has favored the coca plant with a natural pesticide, the alkaloid chemical cocaine, which helps to keep the coca plant alive. The chemical is a potent reuptake inhibitor of the **neurotransmitter** octopamine, which means that coca forces insects to produce too much octopamine, ultimately killing them by overdose.

Coca grows best in warm, moist, frost-free climates, especially at altitudes between 4,921 feet (1,500 meters) and 19,685 feet (6,000 meters) above sea level. The plant can grow as tall as eight feet (2.44 meters), and is usually planted in nurseries, then grown from seed. Harvesting usually begins in the plant's third year; a typical coca bush can then yield three harvests a year for the next twenty years. It is a very resilient plant. Well-cultivated coca plants can be harvestable for up to fifty years.

Coca has grown for centuries on the slopes of the Andes Mountains in Peru, Bolivia, Ecuador, and Colombia.

Cocaine—The Rush to Destruction 17

For centuries, coca chewing has been a part of the culture of South America.

Coca leaves are rich in protein, vitamins, calcium, iron, and fiber. The cocaine content of a leaf varies; factors such as altitude and cultivation method play a large role in determining cocaine content. A coca leaf can contain anywhere from .1 percent to .9 percent cocaine.

For over 5,000 years, South American natives have used cocaine as it naturally occurs in the leaves of *Erythroxylum coca*. Coca chewing reportedly offers the user physical and mental energy. Often the effects of coca chewing are compared to those of caffeine, although coca chewers claim that chewing coca leaves is much more effective as a mood brightener.

Of all the means of consuming cocaine, chewing coca—the most natural (and most ancient) method—produces the mildest effects, which is likely the reason many cocaine abusers choose more potent forms of the drug.

The culture surrounding coca chewing is mostly limited to South America. Coca leaves were used for various social and mythical practices in South American cultures before Europeans arrived, but coca chewing gained popularity when Spanish conquistadors forced many South Americans to work long, hard hours. Such rigorous work needed strong, healthy slaves, and the conquistadors found that slaves worked harder and needed less food or sleep when they were given coca leaves to chew.

Usually, however, coca chewers don't actually chew the leaves. Instead, they are mashed into a paste, moistened with saliva, and tucked between the user's gums and cheek. Often the paste is mixed with lime-rich materials such as burnt seashells or certain cereals.

This is because, in its natural state, most of the cocaine is in a chemical form that is not efficiently absorbed through the lining of the mouth. This is what is called

the "protonated," "ionized," or "bound" form due to the extra proton attached to the molecule. Mixing with alkaline substances removes the proton, resulting in what is called the "unprotonated," "unionized," or "free-base" form of cocaine. Free-base cocaine is rapidly and efficiently absorbed through the lining of the mouth. Saliva that contains cocaine and is swallowed can also result in some absorption but this is relatively slow and inefficient because the cocaine must past through the upper digestive system, where some of it is destroyed.

There are many parallels between oral coca leaf chewing and smokeless tobacco use. In both cases, rapid and more efficient delivery is achieved by added alkaline substances to release the free-base form of the drug. In both cases, swallowing the drug is relatively inefficient in delivering the drug to the brain. And in both cases, the substance can be harmful and highly addictive, but is probably not as likely to produce addiction as smoked forms (for example, crack cocaine or cigarette-delivered nicotine).

Because of the long history of coca chewing without apparent severe adverse physical effects (or scarcity-induced crime due to the plentiful availability in South American countries), some people have advocated for the legal use of coca leaves. Of course, this ignores the facts that even oral

Making cocaine is a complicated and expensive process. The pure-white powder cocaine of Hollywood films takes a long time to create. Here's a basic formula for what it takes to make two pounds of cocaine hydrochloride:

500 to 1,000 pounds of leaves = five pounds of paste = two pounds of cocaine

cocaine is addictive and can produce strong cardiovascular reactions, anorexia, and other adverse physical effects.

Today, many South American natives continue the historical practice of chewing the leaf, and some South American companies have even begun producing a coca beverage called maté de coca. The beverage is generally low in cocaine, and due to the relatively inefficient absorption through the gastrointestinal system, the effects are relatively mild. Those who drink it say the effect is much like coffee. Versions of this, also referred to as "coca tea," have also been used in some cocaine addiction treatment programs as a safer and more controllable

A South American farmer holds coca leaves that he has harvested.

form of cocaine to substitute for smoked and "snorted" forms, though there has been little study of actual safety and effectiveness.

Cocaine Sulfate

Often called pasta, basuco, basa, patillo, or paste, this form of cocaine is considered the lowest grade. Cocaine sulfate is a state between raw coca leaves and finished cocaine hydrochloride crystal. To make this substance, coca leaves are stripped from the plant and then placed into a plastic pit with a solution of water and dilute sulfuric acid. The mixture is then mashed (traditionally by a barefoot man or woman) and laid out to dry, allowing the water to evaporate. What's left is cocaine sulfate, a paste-like substance.

The urban poor of many South American cities comprise the vast majority of cocaine sulfate users. The paste is often combined with marijuana or tobacco and smoked in cigarette form.

Street Names for Cocaine Powder

Bad Rock
Bazooka
Beam
Bernice
Big C
Blast
Blizzard
Blow
Snow Storm

Cocaine Hydrochloride

This salt is the most common form of cocaine, and the one most frequently associated with cocaine in the media. In its purest form, this type of cocaine has a chunk-like texture and is off-white to pink in color. Cocaine hydrochloride

A Very Real Problem

In 2002, an estimated 1.5 million Americans could be classified as dependent on or abusing cocaine in the past twelve months.

In 2005, at least 43,000 Canadian students said they had used cocaine at least once in the past year.

(Source: National Institute for Drug Abuse; Center for Addiction and Mental Health.)

Not So Funny Speedball

In 1982, John Belushi was on a roll. He had had an incredibly successful run on *Saturday Night Live*, but had left the show in 1979 to pursue a career in film. *The Blues Brothers, 1941*, and especially *Animal House*, filmed while he was still a member of *Saturday Night Live*, signaled that his film career was destined for success.

But, that success ended in a Los Angeles hotel room on March 5, 1982. Belushi had a reputation as a drinker and drug user, and a night spent partying would be his last. Earlier in the evening, he partied with actors Robin Williams and Robert DeNiro. After they left, he, a female companion, and perhaps a few other people continued the party. What happened next is somewhat disputed. Some claim that Belushi injected himself with a speedball, a mixture of heroin and cocaine; other reports state that "Cathy Smith," his companion, "shot him up" with the mixture. Regardless, the combination of drugs proved fatal, and Belushi died.

Robin Williams makes no secret that he had a rather "active" drug life during that time. In interviews, he has cited Belushi's death as one of the reasons he made the courageous decision to end his drug use.

Snorting is the most popular method of taking cocaine.

24 Chapter 1—What Is Cocaine?

is *stable* and water-soluble, which makes it possible to drink, inject, or snort it.

Cocaine hydrochloride is frequently diluted with other substances, called "adulterates." Baking soda is the most commonly used adulterate of cocaine hydrochloride, but many substances can be used, some more dangerous than others. By "cutting" cocaine with these additional substances, cocaine dealers are able to charge more money for less pure cocaine; unfortunately, they expose the user to a range of dangers in the process. Nosebleeds, perforated nasal septums, irrational behavior, violence, heart attack, or even sudden death—depending on the substance added, dose, and duration of use—can result from cocaine laced with other substances.

Making cocaine hydrochloride requires a complicated process. Many different substances can be substituted for those in this formula, but the basic process looks something like this: cocaine sulfate is washed in kerosene, then chilled, and then the kerosene removed; gas crystals of crude cocaine remain; the crystals are dissolved in methyl alcohol, then recrystalized and dissolved once again in sulfuric acid. The process is completed with washing, *oxidation*, and separation procedures that use potassium permanganate, benzole, and sodium carbonate. The salt-like final product is what most people visualize when they hear the word "cocaine."

Cocaine hydrochloride has typically been snorted in the Western world, and sometimes injected. Snorting is most popular, but it is actually a less effective method. The mucus membranes inside the nasal cavity and sinuses absorb the powder, but only about 30 to 40 percent of the cocaine reaches the bloodstream and is carried to the brain. This inefficient delivery is partially the result

Crack is usually heated on a piece of tinfoil.

of **vasoconstriction**, an effect of snorting cocaine that closes up the nasal passages and over time, destroys the nasal septum.

Because they deliver more powerful effects, free-base and crack cocaine have become increasingly popular among users.

Free-Base Cocaine

This form of cocaine is not only extremely addictive but also quite dangerous to make. The procedure to make free-base cocaine involves ether, an extremely flammable substance. Free-base cocaine is insoluble in water, and it can't be injected or swallowed. It does, however, vaporize at a low temperature, making it suitable for inhalation, which gives the user an immediate, intense high; the rush comes more quickly than injection and is more intense, lasting around five minutes.

Crack Cocaine

Because of the inconvenience and danger of using ether, crack cocaine evolved as a more popular way to inhale cocaine. To make crack cocaine, all one must do is skip the free-base step of removing pure cocaine from the base mixture; instead, one takes the impure cocaine "rock" and heats it, inhaling the evaporating fumes. Because water and a **base** such as baking soda are a part of the crack mixture, the rock tends to crackle when heated, giving it the name "crack."

Crack is most often smoked, usually heated in a pipe or on a piece of tin foil; sometimes it is mixed with tobacco or marijuana in a joint. The euphoric rush usually lasts no longer than thirty minutes. Crack may be safer to

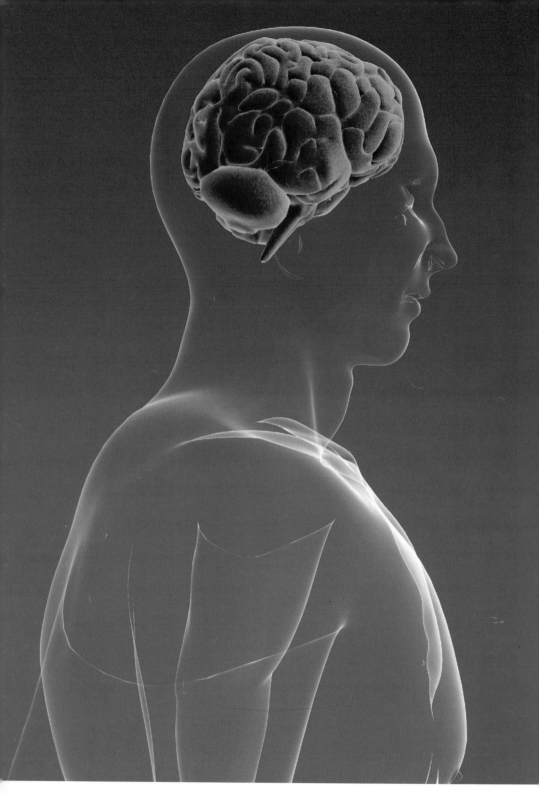

Cocaine has many negative effects on the central nervous system, particularly the brain.

produce than free-base cocaine, but it is certainly no less addictive. Both offer users a temporary high that leaves them craving more.

Why Is Cocaine So Addictive?

Cocaine is an extremely powerful psychostimulant. Substances like cocaine are called "stimulants" because they stimulate the central nervous system (CNS), which includes the brain and spinal cord. In doing so, the person's thoughts and actions become faster, as though the person's brain and body had been put into fast forward. The sensation is often pleasurable, but there is a steep price to pay for this pleasure. Thinking can become disordered, producing errors in judgement and sometimes violence.

Cocaine has the ability to send the CNS into a vicious, downward spiral of addiction. It creates a desire that can only be satisfied by more cocaine abuse, and destroys, rather than creates, any sense of permanent satisfaction

It took thousands of years before the first scientist isolated the alkaloid from the coca plant, however. The history of cocaine is important in fully understanding the powerful drug it has become today.

2 The History of Cocaine

Imagine this:

You haven't slept or eaten anything for two days. Your body is shaking all over from sleep deprivation, thirst, and hunger—but you're giddy with happiness. You've just scored your next hit. You snatch the forty-dollar bag from your dealer's hand and start to open it right there, standing behind the counter of a nightclub bar, but he stops you.

"Don't do that in here" he says.

Your hands are trembling by now, anticipating the hit as you stumble out the back door, unwrap the plastic bag, and place one of the brownish-white rocks into your cracked glass pipe. When the hit comes, it comes fast. If someone asked you how many rocks you've smoked in the past two days of your crack binge, you wouldn't be

Machu Picchu, one of the Inca's ancient sacred cities, would have seen its share of coca use by the priests who dwelled here.

able to tell them exactly—but considering you spent almost 400 hundred dollars yesterday, and then begged or stole to buy the rest today, you estimate you've smoked too many.

As you slouch down contentedly against the side of the alley, you feel like you own the whole world. You're a free person because you don't need a thing but the cocaine in your lungs right now.

Then it starts to happen: the hunger pangs return, and the world comes ticking back toward you. It's only a matter of time, after all.

You reach for the plastic bag.

This is just a brief description of what many crack addicts have called "hell on earth"—an intense period of psychological craving for crack cocaine, often called a "crack binge." Crack addiction is one of the most publicized addictions, and yet crack is in its babyhood compared to the history of cocaine.

The Incan Empire and Coca

Thousands of years ago, coca had a sacred status. It was considered a holy plant, scattered by priests during religious ceremonies for the gods. Often the mouths of deceased royalty would be filled with coca for the journey to the next world. Coca played an important role in Incan weddings, funerals, and the *huaraca*, or initiation rite for young Incan nobles.

Coca—as well as other useful plants like maize—was thought to have a divine essence, its "mother," Mama Coca. In Incan myths, Mama Coca is always pictured as a beautiful woman; one of the Incan rulers actually gave his wife the name Mama Coca. Because coca was so highly esteemed, reserved for royalty and priests, it was rarely available to the common people. The Incan elite maintained most of the coca in *cocales*, coca plantations reserved for special occasions. Archaeological evidence suggests that the common masses did use coca ceremonially and as a medicine, but it was not until the Spanish conquest that its daily use became popular.

The Spanish Conquerors

The newly arrived Spanish were initially hostile to coca. At formal councils in 1551 and 1567, the leaders of the Catholic Church determined coca chewing to be a form of **idolatry**; a similar royal proclamation declared coca a demoniacal illusion. Ironically, at the time these declarations were issued in Europe, Spaniards across the Atlantic in the New World were already putting coca to use in their silver and gold mines and plantations.

The Spanish quickly realized coca was useful for keeping Incans working longer and harder. Diets were often poor in the regions where the Spanish were mining and cultivating cash crops, so the introduction of coca into a worker's diet could allow him to work longer with less food and water. The Spanish noticed this, and encouraged the natives to use coca daily.

The technique was really nothing new; for many years, South American natives in Peru had used coca for stamina. It was common practice in these mountain cultures to send runners long distances to deliver messages, with coca leaves serving as the messenger's only nourishment.

Eventually, the Church condoned the cultivation of coca but maintained **sanctions** on its religious use. The

An artist's portrayal of a Spanish conquistador's first glimpse of "Mama Coca."

Vin Mariani

Angelo Mariani made his fortune from the coca-wine sold as Vin Mariani. Advertisements for the beverage were aimed at both upper and lower classes, often featuring subtle sexuality to entice the consumer. One advertisement read,

Vin Mariani,
Popular French Tonic Wine:
Fortifies and refreshes body and brain!
Restores health and vitality!

The drink was so popular that Pope Leo XIII was reported to carry a hipflask of the drink with him at all times. The grateful pope would later award Mariani a Vatican gold medal to show his appreciation for the drink.

Church had overwhelming incentive to do so, as the taxes on coca actually provided the clergy with much of their revenue. The Spanish royalty followed suit, issuing an order under Viceroy Francisco de Toledo in 1573 that removed obstacles to the cultivation of coca.

Eventually, coca would become a major player on the world stage.

Coca in Europe

Years went by before Europeans took any major interest in the South American plant. Coca had yet to prove its usefulness to Europeans, and cocaine had yet to be isolated from the coca leaf. Europe was skeptical of coca. It took many travelers' tales of the benefits of coca and the work of a few scientists to create a change in attitudes toward coca in Europe.

Because coca leaves deteriorate quickly, very few made it across the seas for scientific study. It wasn't until

Pope Leo XIII, who ruled the Catholic Church in the nineteenth century, carried a hip flask of coca wine with him at all times to keep him "refreshed."

Cocaine—The Rush to Destruction 37

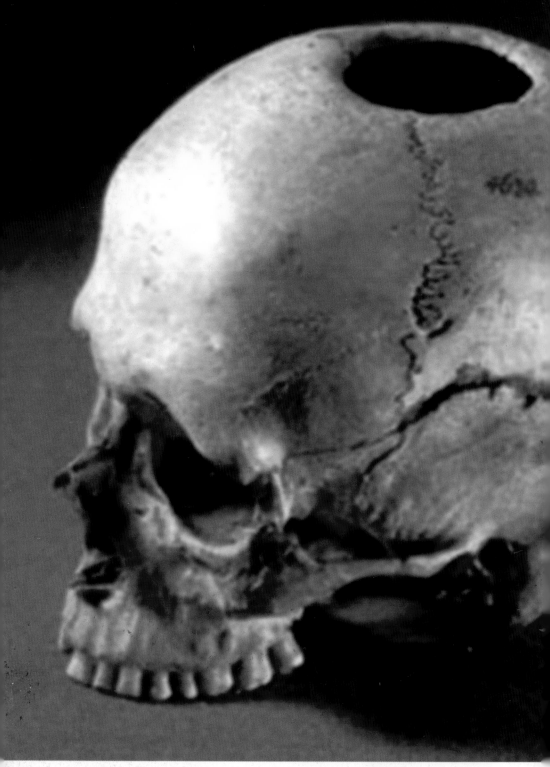

Many ancient skulls from South America have been found with holes in them, indicating that complicated surgery took place, probably with coca used as anesthesia.

the nineteenth century that Europe began to know the properties of coca that might substantiate the claims of travelers. One such traveler to South America was Paolo Mantegazza, a nineteenth-century neurologist who lavished coca with praise, and whose writings on coca would eventually be influential on Sigmund Freud's experimentation with cocaine. Mantegazza wrote, "I prefer a life of ten years with coca to one of a hundred thousand without it."

It 1855, Friedrich Gaedcke produced a crystalline extract from coca that he called "Erythroxylin." It was probably a mixture of many alkaloids, only one of which was cocaine. The rest happened quickly: in 1860, Albert Niemann finally isolated the primary cocaine alkaloid; in 1862, Wilhelm Lossen discovered the chemical formula for cocaine; a few years later, scientists isolated the other coca alkaloids. These scientists never guessed where their discoveries would lead.

Throughout the nineteenth century, both coca and cocaine were used medicinally and recreationally in Europe. South American cultures had long known that coca had medical uses, and archaeological evidence suggests that natives were aware of cocaine's anesthetic properties. Numerous skulls have been discovered in South America with holes drilled in them, a sign that complicated surgery was possible because of the anesthetic properties of coca. In 1859, Mantegazza recommended coca for toothache, digestive disorders, and other illnesses; in 1863, Angelo Mariani, a Corsican chemist, created a concoction of coca extract and wine that he called "Vin Mariani."

The 1870s and 1880s saw cocaine further integrated into European culture. In 1884, two influential events

In 1986, Boston Celtics draft pick Len Bias and football's Don Rogers of the Cleveland Browns both died from cocaine use, proving that just one dose could be lethal even to healthy young athletes. Shortly after Bias's death, the Senate's Permanent Subcommittee on Investigations held a hearing on crack cocaine. During the hearing's debate, senators cited Bias's death eleven times. By the fall, Congress had adopted the Anti-Drug Abuse Act, which included harsh new mandatory sentences for low-level crack offenses. Defendants convicted with just 5 grams of crack cocaine, the weight of five sugar packets, were subject to a five-year mandatory minimum sentence.

accelerated the rise in the popularity of coca: Freud's paper "On Coca" and Karl Koller's rediscovery of cocaine's anesthetic properties. Freud had conducted research and determined that coca should be considered a stimulant, like caffeine, and not a narcotic, like opium. He tried using cocaine as a "treatment" to help him give up cigar smoking; unfortunately, the treatment proved unsuccessful. Koller's discovery was particularly successful in the field of ophthalmology, as patients undergoing eye surgery often needed to remain conscious during the operation. Cocaine, it turned out, was a very good anesthetic for eye surgery, and was happily used to replace ether, which often caused vomiting and was hazardous to the patient.

Cocaine in the United States

By the 1880s, cocaine was being freely distributed by physicians for maladies such as exhaustion, depression, and even to treat morphine addiction. The drug was available in many medicinal forms. Coca-containing tonics, elixirs, and powders were sold throughout the United States with a wide variety of promises: "cocaine can cure your cough" or "cocaine sooths sore throats!" Most of these early cocaine concoctions were not wholly misleading,

An advertisement for Vin Mariania, the concoction of wine and coca extract, claimed that the product "fortified and refreshed."

Fighting Crack

In San Francisco, California, the crack epidemic reached its peak around 1989. Every night, dozens of people (mostly young men) were hauled off the streets for buying and selling crack, and then put back onto the streets a few days later. It seemed like an endless cycle until the women of the "Prevention Pot" program arrived on the streets.

No one knew what to make of the teapot-wielding women at first—most of them were elderly; a few addicts even recognized their grandmothers among the women. The anxious crack addicts lined up for cups of hot tea poured in Styrofoam cups, and were surprised by the warm confidence that filled them with each sip. After an hour or so, the women packed up their pots, but returned later that afternoon with more of the refreshing brew. Before long, tea was replacing crack vials.

It took the San Francisco police department a few weeks to figure out why calls from that neighborhood had decreased by 60 percent: the women of Prevention Pot were selling a coca-leaf tea. Although initially the government was concerned one addiction was being replaced by another, time and experience showed the benefits of coca tea (coined "cokee") far outweighed the hazards.

as cocaine does have a numbing effect and is a powerful stimulant, but the "miracle drug" status cocaine was achieving was deceptive at best.

In 1885, John Pemberton from Georgia developed a new product—French Wine Coca, Ideal Nerve and Tonic Stimulant. The concoction was derived from South American coca leaves and cola nuts; it sold for a nickel per eight-ounce bottle, and it contained a good 60 milligrams of cocaine. However, since Pemberton's name for his new beverage was a bit of a mouthful, the following year he shortened it to something more catchy—Coca-Cola.

John Pemberton was the inventor of the original Coca-Cola.

A calendar from 1901 advertised an early form of "the real stuff."

Back in those days, Coke certainly *was* the "real thing." Mr. Pemberton described it this way:

This "Intellectual Beverage" and Temperance Drink . . . makes not only a delicious, exhilarating, refreshing and invigorating Beverage . . . but a valuable Brain Tonic, and a cure for all nervous affections—Sick Head-ache, Neuralgia, Hysteria, Melancholy, &c.

The peculiar flavor of COCA-COLA delights every palate; it is dispensed from the soda fountain in same manner as any of the fruit syrups.

Cocaine did indeed make its users feel good—at least temporarily—and it was used in nineteenth-century America for a variety of ailments. Even Abraham Lincoln, shortly before the 1860 presidential election, purchased a bottle of cocaine for fifty cents at a drugstore; among its many other abilities, cocaine was thought to help grow beards.

By 1890, however, the medical and scientific community had become suspicious of the addictive and harmful properties of cocaine abuse. Still, it wasn't until 1906, when the Pure Food and Drug Act was passed, that the federal government took any action against cocaine. The act prohibited interstate shipment of food and soda water containing cocaine, and required products containing the drug to be properly labeled as doing so The act proved somewhat effective, but ultimately the Harrison Narcotic Act, passed in 1914, would be the definitive law on cocaine in the United States. It required anyone handling the drug to be registered with the federal government, and it made cocaine available to citizens by a physician's prescription only. Under the new law, unregistered persons in possession of cocaine violated regulatory and tax provisions, and were subject to prosecution.

Over the next few years, and with the prompting of the United States, many European countries passed laws similar to the Harrison Narcotic Act. In 1922, Congress prohibited the importation of almost all coca and cocaine, and in 1932, the Uniform Narcotics Act was passed; not much was done to the law until the 1950s, when punishment for possession was made more severe.

During the years in between, the smuggling of cocaine into North America was limited, and the **black market** for cocaine was still small. **Amphetamines** ruled as drug of choice for most substance abusers until the late 1960s, when the federal government began to crack down on them. At that point, cocaine regained popularity. During the 1970s, cocaine was usually sniffed in its hydrochloride, powdered form, as it had been in the early twentieth century. As cocaine abusers realized the inefficacy of snorting, some "graduated" to intravenous use. It wasn't until the 1980s, that a smokable form of cocaine was readily available: crack cocaine.

History of Crack

Until the 1970s and 1980s, cocaine was in many ways a drug of the upper class. Because production and isolation of the drug is so complicated, the price for cocaine has remained high throughout its history, and so in the early twentieth century it was sometimes a symbol of status if one possessed cocaine. In the 1950s and 1960s, as other forms of drug abuse escalated, cocaine abuse and addiction remained relatively uncommon due to the very

Cocaine's most common form is a white powder.

In urban areas, gangs formed around the buying and selling of crack.

limited access and high cost of pure forms of the drugs. But all of that changed with the escalation of South American product distribution to the United States. Seemingly out of nowhere, relatively pure forms of cocaine could be obtained almost anywhere and at low cost, with unit doses eventually dropping to less than ten dollars in many regions. This facilitated the introduction of crack because although crack is very effective at producing rapid and powerful effects, it "wastes" some of the drug through the manufacturing and burning process.

Free-base was relatively difficult to produce from cocaine hydrochloride, and more dangerous; crack was safer and easier to make. Crack also produced the illusion of having more of the drug, as bases (most commonly baking soda) often comprised the majority of crack rocks. It could be packaged conveniently in paper pouches. These were often decorated and labeled, allowing distributors to schieve "brand recognition."

This new form of cocaine could be smoked, it was more addictive, and it was cheaper to produce, giving crack a "downmarket" appeal. Crack became popular among the urban poor, and gangs often formed around the buying and selling of crack cocaine.

Communities around the country responded quickly to crack cocaine, calling for government intervention and increased attention to the problem of crack. Because of these strong efforts, total cocaine consumption between the years of 1985 and 1999 is estimated to have decreased by 70 percent.

Cocaine Timeline

c.3000 BCE.	Coca chewing becomes popular among the people of the Andes.
1400 CE	The Inca people of Peru farm coca.
Early 1500s	Inca coca plantations are taken over by Spanish invaders. Spanish authorities tax coca production. Reports of the properties of the coca leaf reach Europe.
c.1575	Laborers in South American silver mines are given coca leaves as payment.
1708	Coca is included in a dictionary of medicinal plants by Herman Boerhaave of Germany.
1855	Cocaine is extracted from coca leaves by German scientist Friedrich Gaedcke.
1859	The extraction process is improved by Albert Niemann.
1862	E. Merck Company produces a quarter-pound of refined cocaine.
1869	Seeds of the coca plant become part of the botanical collection at Kew Gardens, London.
1880	Russian doctor Vasili von Anrep discovers the anesthetizing properties of cocaine.
1884	Cocaine is first used as a local anesthetic in eye surgery. The psychiatrist Sigmund Freud publishes his ideas about cocaine in a paper called "On Coca."
1886	Coca-Cola, containing cocaine syrup and caffeine, is launched onto the market.
1905	Snorting cocaine becomes fashionable.

1909	Cocaine is used on the Antarctic expedition of Sir Ernest Shackleton.
1910	Medical journals report cases of nasal damage due to snorting cocaine.
1911	U.S. government reports 5,000 cocaine-related deaths.
1924	Second International Opium Conference at The Hague includes cocaine in a list of drugs that should have their production and use reduced.
1976	Freebase cocaine is developed.
1980s	Crack cocaine is developed. Crack and freebase become popular.
2002	The U.S. Department of Health and Human Services reports that the number of adolescents using illicit drugs declined from 15 percent in 1997 to 9.7 percent in 2000.

(*Source:* Sarah Lennard-Brown's "Cocaine Timeline.")

Drug Use Around the World

Drug	% of World Population (over age 15) using drug
all illegal drugs	4.2%
marijuana	3.3%
amphetamines	0.7%
cocaine	0.3%

(*Source:* United Nations Office on Drugs and Crime World Drug Report 2000.)

3 What Are the Dangers of Cocaine?

In order to understand the effects of cocaine on the body, we must first examine how cocaine works in the brain. Cocaine has a powerful impact on the brain's functions. All cocaine's effects (euphoria, decreased appetite, alertness, and increased ability to concentrate) occur because the drug stimulates a group of chemicals called monoamine neurotransmitters.

Neurotransmitters, the messengers between different nerves in your body, and nerves and neurons are the primary components of the body's complex communication system. If your brain wants your hand to move from its position on your lap to the pencil on your desk, a complex system of nerves is activated to send that message. Though it seems easy enough to do, that simple action requires a distinct language to communicate between nerves, and the neurotransmitters serve as that language. Neurons do not touch each other, and the area between the neurons is called the synapse. Messages are sent when

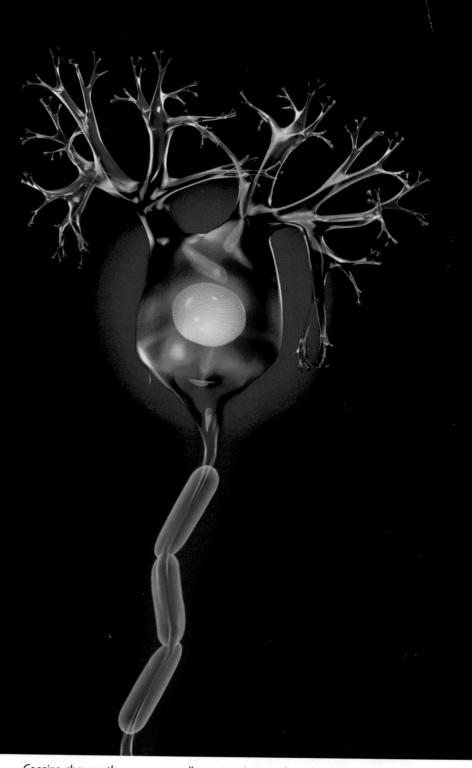

Cocaine changes the way nerve cells communicate with each other.

Cocaine is a strong central nervous system stimulant that interferes with the reabsorption process of dopamine, a chemical messenger associated with pleasure and movement. The buildup of dopamine causes continuous stimulation of receiving neurons, which is associated with the euphoria commonly reported by cocaine abusers.

(*Source:* National Institute on Drug Abuse.)

the impulse reaches the end of the neuron, catches a ride across the synapse on a neurotransmitter, and arrives at the next neuron. Cocaine increases the amounts of neurotransmitters serotonin, noradrenaline, and dopamine in the synapse, which excites the nerve endings and sends out more signals. This can make the cocaine user feel excited, powerful, and full of energy, depending on which neurotransmitter is affected.

Serotonin

Serotonin plays a large role in controlling your body's internal clock. Body temperature, sleep cycle, and appetite are all affected by serotonin. An unnatural amount of serotonin in someone's body can make them extremely sleepy when they should be alert, or anxious and alert when they should be going to sleep. When properly controlled, serotonin should make you feel hungry at times when your body is used to being fed, such as breakfast, lunch, and dinner, but the cocaine user may experience total appetite loss for days.

Noradrenaline (or Norepinephrine)

This chemical *hormone* is one of many produced during a state of shock. Noradrenaline helps regulate a proper response to emergency; it prepares your body to fight or

Signs a Teen May Be on Cocaine

- red eyes
- runny nose or frequent sniffing
- change of eating habits and loss of weight
- change of sleeping habits; sleeps all day and is up all night
- a change in friends and groups within different ages
- a change in behaviors, such as flunking out of school or not going to school
- frequently needing money and stealing it to support her habit
- losing interest in the things he used to like to do, such as family activities
- acting withdrawn or depressed, very tired and careless about personal appearance

(*Source*: www.teendrugabuse.us/teen_cocaine_use.html.)

escape—the fight-or-flight response. Noradrenalin makes more energy available to your brain and muscles, and widens passages in your lungs to allow more oxygen to enter your body. Noradrenalin can also reduce appetite, as the body makes hunger a low priority during its fight-or-flight response. The "rush" and excitement of cocaine are due to the stimulation of this chemical hormone.

Dopamine

Dopamine is the chemical in your brain related to happiness. Scientists and doctors include dopamine in what they call the "reward system" of the brain; when the brain lacks dopamine, you feel sad; when the brain has an excess of dopamine, you feel very happy. According to the reward system, dopamine reinforces the feelings achieved during pleasurable experiences such as laughing, eating, or exercising. Our brains are thought to have evolved a system of rewards and pleasure that responds to behaviors that help us survive. Unfortunately, cocaine directly activates these same circuits and helps to essentially condition or stamp in behaviors that are not only not necessary for survival but behaviors that can be highly destructive, leading to compulsive cocaine use, as well as other maladaptive behaviors to obtain cocaine, including crime and deception.

Once cocaine is broken down by a user's system, the overproduction of neurotransmitters halts, and the normal production of neurotransmitters is reduced; after experiencing unnaturally high levels of activity, the brain

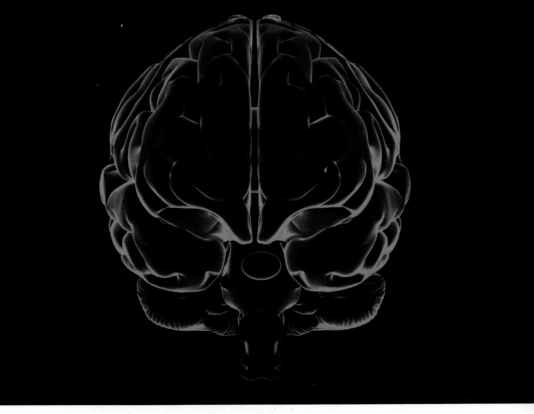

Chemicals within the human brain are responsible for emotions.

Short-Term Dangers

Cocaine's effects appear almost immediately after a single dose and disappear within a few minutes or hours. Taken in small amounts (up to 100 mg), cocaine usually makes the user feel euphoric, energetic, talkative, and mentally alert, especially to the sensations of sight, sound, and touch. It can also produce wakefulness and lack of appetite. Some users find that the drug helps them perform simple physical and intellectual tasks more quickly, while others experience the opposite effect. Prolonged use can be highly debilitating in either case.

The duration of cocaine's immediate euphoric effects depends upon the route of administration: the faster the absorption, the more intense the high. Also, the faster the absorption, the shorter the duration of action. The high from snorting is relatively slow in onset, and may last 15 to 30 minutes, while that from smoking may last 5 to 10 minutes.

The short-term physiological effects of cocaine include constricted blood vessels; dilated pupils; and increased temperature, heart rate, and blood pressure. Large amounts (several hundred milligrams or more) intensify the user's high, but may also lead to bizarre, erratic, and violent behavior. These users may experience tremors, vertigo, muscle twitches, paranoia, or, with repeated doses, a toxic reaction closely resembling amphetamine poisoning. Some users of cocaine report feelings of restlessness, irritability, and anxiety. In rare instances, sudden death can occur on the first use of cocaine or unexpectedly thereafter. Cocaine-related deaths are often a result of cardiac arrest or seizures followed by respiratory arrest.

(*Source*: National Institute on Drug Abuse.)

now experiences unnaturally low levels of activity accompanied by lethargy and loss of self-confidence. The cocaine abuser may force himself to forget these post-cocaine lows, remembering only the initial rush or the sense of euphoria, but eventually these lows will lead to severe unhappiness and addiction as cocaine becomes the only escape for the dopamine-deficient abuser.

Cocaine users experience an initial "rush" that is often followed by periods of depression.

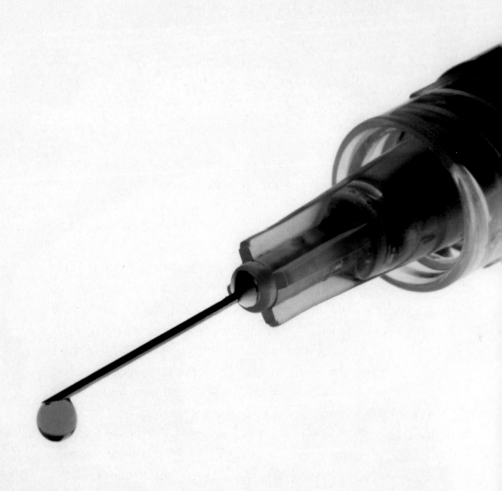

Injecting cocaine increases the risk of overdose; when needles are shared, the chance of contracting a disease such as HIV or hepatitis is an added risk.

Cocaine Addiction

Usually, an addiction to cocaine takes time to develop, but many addicts have reported psychological addiction from the first hit. Changes in a person happen slowly, as her body adapts to the increasingly familiar presence of cocaine. The human body will adjust to increased levels of dopamine by minimizing the amounts of dopamine it naturally produces. Less available dopamine makes the cocaine user less able to experience pleasure from normal activities, and less able to experience pleasure from the drug the next time they use it. More cocaine is needed to get high, tolerance develops, and the addiction process has begun.

Crack cocaine accelerates this process. Because the pleasure of a hit is so intense, but only lasts upward of fifteen minutes, the crack cocaine user enters the cycle of addiction quickly: more hits, more frequently, with less time in between for the body to adjust its dopamine production to normal levels. The crack user can become maniacal, centering his life around crack cocaine without regard for food, sleep, or safety—all three of which have become irrelevant, failing to provide any pleasure. All cocaine users—not just crack cocaine users—experience feelings of depression and **melancholy** after cocaine use.

Dangers of Injecting Cocaine

The danger of overdosing is always present when injecting cocaine. In addition, complications are associated with sharing needles and syringes.

Disease

Sharing equipment can pass on infections such as HIV and hepatitis B and C from one person to another. Hepatitis B is a serious disease caused by a virus that attacks the liver. The virus, which is called hepatitis B virus (HBV), can cause lifelong infection, cirrhosis (scarring) of the liver, liver cancer, liver failure, and death. Hepatitis C is a liver disease caused by the hepatitis C virus (HCV), which is found in the blood of persons who have the disease. HCV is spread by contact with the blood of an infected person. A drop of blood so minuscule that it cannot be detected by the human eye may contain hundreds or even thousands of hepatitis B and/or C particles. Even meticulous cleaning may not totally eradicate from a needle the viruses that cause these serious liver diseases.

Tetanus (sometimes referred to as lockjaw) is a serious but preventable disease that affects the body's muscles and nerves. It is usually spread from a skin wound that becomes contaminated by a bacterium that is often found in soil. Most cases of tetanus in North America follow a cut or deep puncture injury, such as a wound caused by stepping on a nail—but skin punctures from nonsterile needles (such as with drug use) can also spread the bacteria. Once the bacteria are in the body, they produce a neurotoxin (a protein that acts as a poison to the body's nervous system) that causes muscle spasms. The toxin first affects nerves controlling the muscles near the wound, but it can also travel to other parts of the body through the bloodstream and lymph system. As it circulates through the body, the toxin interferes with the normal activity of nerves, leading to generalized muscle spasms. Without treatment, tetanus can be fatal.

HIV/AIDS is also a possibility that is all too common for users who inject cocaine. HIV stands for the human immunodeficiency virus, a retrovirus. Retroviruses integrate and take over a cell's own genetic material. Once taken over, the new cell, now infected with HIV, begins

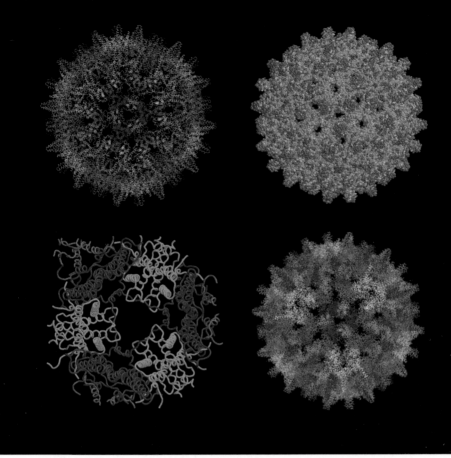

A single drop of blood may contain thousands of hepatitis B particles like these.

to produce new HIV retroviruses. HIV replicates in the T cells, the body's main defense against illness, and eventually kills them. HIV is only spread through:

- Sexual contact from unprotected (without using a condom) vaginal or anal sex.
- Direct inoculation of the virus through contaminated needles.
- Contaminated blood products/transplanted organs. (In the United States, all donated blood has been tested for HIV since 1985.)
- An infected mother may sometimes pass the virus to her developing fetus during the birth or through her breast milk.

Long-Term Dangers

There can be severe medical complications associated with cocaine use. Some of the most frequent complications are cardiovascular effects, including disturbances in heart rhythm and heart attacks; respiratory effects such as chest pain and respiratory failure; neurological effects, including strokes, seizures, and headaches; and gastrointestinal complications, including abdominal pain and nausea.

Cocaine use has been linked to many types of heart disease. Cocaine has been found to trigger chaotic heart rhythms, called ventricular fibrillation; accelerate heartbeat and breathing; and increase blood pressure and body temperature. Physical symptoms may include chest pain, nausea, blurred vision, fever, muscle spasms, convulsions, coma, and death.

Different routes of cocaine administration can produce different adverse effects. Regularly snorting cocaine, for example, can lead to loss of sense of smell, nosebleeds, problems with swallowing, hoarseness, and an overall irritation of the nasal septum, which can lead to a chronically inflamed, runny nose. Ingested cocaine can cause severe bowel gangrene, due to reduced blood flow. And, persons who inject cocaine have puncture marks and "tracks," most commonly in their forearms. Intravenous cocaine users may also experience an allergic reaction, either to the drug, or to some additive in street cocaine, which can result, in severe cases, in death. Because cocaine has a tendency to decrease food intake, many chronic cocaine users lose their appetites and can experience significant weight loss and malnourishment.

Research has revealed a potentially dangerous interaction between cocaine and alcohol. Taken in combination, the two drugs are converted by the body to cocaethylene. Cocaethylene has a longer duration of action in the brain and is more toxic than either drug alone. While more research needs to be done, it is noteworthy that the mixture of cocaine and alcohol is the most common two-drug combination that results in drug-related death.

(*Source*: National Institute on Drug Abuse.)

The first one to three months after a person is initially infected with the HIV virus is when that person is most *infectious* (that is, the amount of virus in her system is at its highest and T-cell counts are at their lowest). During this time, the body has not had time to react to the virus and produce an adequate immune response to start suppressing HIV. More and more HIV viruses are produced and then released by a process known as budding. This means that when someone becomes infected with the HIV virus, it begins to attack his immune system. This process is not visible, and a person who is infected can look and feel perfectly well for many years; she may not even know that she is infected. As the immune system weakens, however, the person will become more vulnerable to illnesses that the immune system would normally have been able to fight. As time goes by, individuals with HIV are likely to become ill more often and develop AIDS.

AIDS stands for acquired immunodeficiency syndrome. When HIV infection becomes advanced, it often is referred to as AIDS. It is characterized by the appearance of *opportunistic* infections that take advantage of a weakened immune system and include:

- *pneumocystis carinii pneumonia*
- *toxoplasmosis*
- *tuberculosis*
- extreme weight loss and wasting, often made worse by diarrhea
- meningitis and other brain infections
- fungal infections
- syphilis
- malignancies such as *lymphoma*, cervical cancer, and *Kaposi's sarcoma*

Short-Term Effects of Cocaine

- euphoria
- depression
- anxiety
- tremors
- accelerated heartbeat
- risk of heart failure and stroke
- headache
- faster breathing
- energy
- illusion of strength

Long-Term Effects of Cocaine

- infections
- severe damage to nasal septum (strip of tissue between two nostrils)
- depression
- anxiety
- heart disease
- stroke
- hallucinations
- malnutrition
- psychosis, sometimes resulting in erratic and violent behavior
- infertility

Cocaine Overdose

- irregular heartbeat
- convulsions
- heart failure
- respiratory arrest
- coma
- death

AIDS—acquired immunodeficiency syndrome—derived its name because:

- It is "acquired"; in other words, it is a condition that has to be **contracted**. It cannot be inherited or transmitted through the genes.
- It affects the body's immune system, the part of the body that fights off diseases.
- It is considered a "deficiency" because it makes the immune system stop working properly.
- It was originally considered a syndrome because people with AIDS experience a number of different symptoms and opportunistic diseases.

Although nearly everyone in the world knows the term acquired immunodeficiencysyndrome or AIDS, this condition is actually a disease and not a syndrome. A syndrome is commonly used to refer to collections of symptoms that do not have an easily identifiable cause; when the term AIDS was first used, doctors were only aware of the late stages of the disease and did not fully understand its mechanisms. A more current name for the condition, regardless of an AIDS diagnosis, is HIV disease. This name is more accurate because it refers to the **pathogen** that causes AIDS and encompasses all the

> **Fast Fact**
>
> Among students surveyed as part of the 2005 Monitoring the Future study, 3.7 percent of eighth-graders, 5.2 percent of tenth-graders, and 8.0 percent of twelfth-graders reported trying cocaine at least once in their lives.

The MTF Survey

Since 1975, the Monitoring the Future (MTF) survey has measured drug, alcohol, and cigarette use and related attitudes among adolescent students nationwide. Survey participants report their drug use behaviors across three time periods: lifetime, past year, and past month. In 2005, 49,347 students in grades 8, 10, and 12 from 402 public and private schools participated in the survey. The survey is funded by the National Institute on Drug Abuse, a component of the National Institutes of Health, and conducted by the University of Michigan.

condition's stages, from infection to the deterioration of the immune system and the onset of opportunistic diseases. However, AIDS is still the name that most people use to refer to the immune deficiency caused by HIV. It is a real and deadly danger for cocaine users who exchange needles.

Other disease dangers caused by injecting cocaine include endocarditis (an infection of the heart), septicemia (a deadly infection of the blood), and gangrene (a bacterial infection that destroys tissue). When the same injection site is used repeatedly, the surrounding tissue matter can also be destroyed, deadening it in a process called necrosis. Repeated abuse of veins and tissue can also lead to blood clots in the veins (thrombosis) and inflammation of veins (phlebitis).

Some countries have developed programs to distribute clean needles to addicts, with the hope that HIV and other diseases will decline among the drug community.

Dangers of Maternal Cocaine Use

The unborn child of a mother addicted to cocaine faces an array of dangers before entering the world. Although more research is needed to determine the full range of

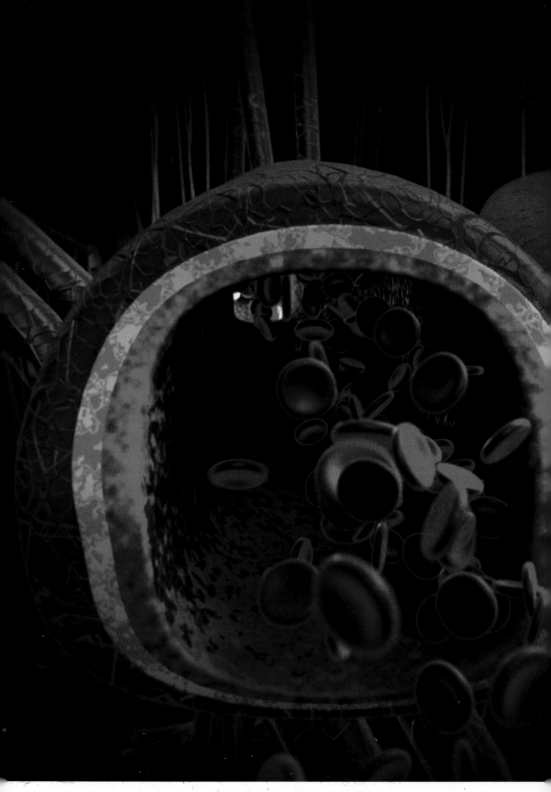

Injecting cocaine can cause infections of the heart and blood.

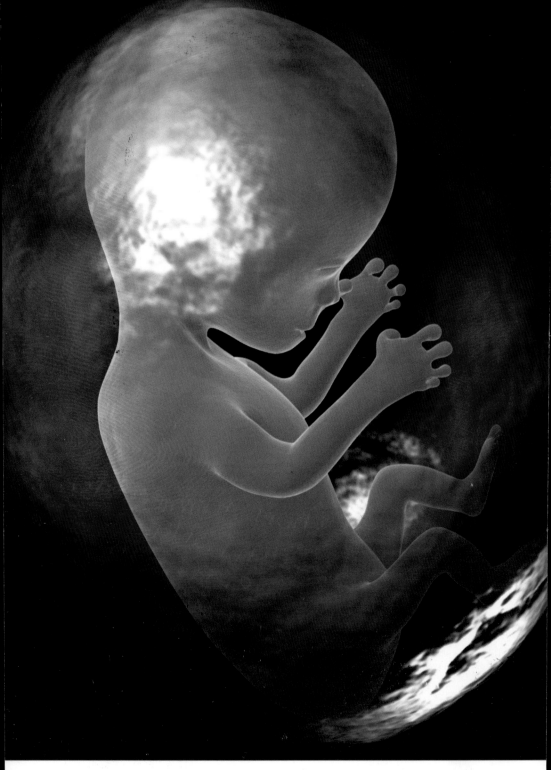

When a pregnant woman uses cocaine, she is likely to damage the developing
fetus.

Cocaine and Needles in Canada

In Canada, the most commonly injected drugs are cocaine and heroin. This is a cause for concern in itself, as cocaine use involves particular risk. Persons who inject cocaine inject as often as twenty times a day, increasing the problems associated with obtaining clean needles and sharing contaminated needles.

The proportion of people who report sharing needles varies considerably, but is exceedingly high in many communities: 76 percent in Montreal, 69 percent in Vancouver, 64 percent in a semi-rural Nova Scotia community, 54 percent in Quebec City and Calgary, 46 percent in Toronto, and 37 percent in Hamilton-Wentworth.

(Source: Public Health Agency of Canada.)

the drug's impact, scientific studies have determined that children born to a cocaine-abusing mother are often prematurely delivered, have lower birth weights, smaller head circumferences, and are shorter in length.

Recent studies have shown that these children often face subtle but significant challenges throughout their development:

- less-than-average cognitive performance
- information-processing difficulties
- trouble paying attention for extended periods of time.

These are all challenges to a child's education and can severely inhibit growth.

In spite of the risks, people continue to experiment with and abuse cocaine.

The Cocaine Trend

According to recent statistical research, cocaine use among twelfth-graders never returned to its peak in the

Cocaine addiction affects males and females of all ages and all socioeconomic groups.

mid-1980s; it has, however, increased from its low point in the early 1990s. In a poll taken in 1985, 17.1 percent of twelfth-graders admitted to taking cocaine at least once in their lifetime. In 2005, 8.0 percent of twelfth-graders said they'd tried cocaine at least once.

Cocaine abuse affects both genders and many different socioeconomic populations across the country. According to surveys done in 2005, males are one and a half to two times more likely to use cocaine than females. In the United States, beginning in the 1970s, cocaine was a drug primarily of the upper classes; in the mid-1980s, however, with the arrival of cheaper, more effective crack cocaine, the *demographic* changed. Crack cocaine was made available for as little as ten dollars, and a culture of illegal selling and gang violence grew alongside crack cocaine.

It's important to remember that anyone can become addicted to cocaine—regardless of age, income, gender, or race—because it is a powerfully addictive drug. But it's equally important to remember that a lot fewer people use cocaine than you might guess, based on its high profile in the media.

4 Issues Surrounding Cocaine

Despite how it is sometimes portrayed in the media, cocaine is not a glamorous drug. Its abuse is not exclusive, nor is it a drug of the elite. Though cocaine use in North America has greatly declined since the 1980s, cocaine continues to be abused, confusing many people. Cocaine is a dangerous, expensive drug that offers little in return for its price; the high fades quickly, and addiction can take hold from the first few hits. Even so, cocaine continues to be bought and sold, and its persistent presence in the drug world has caused a variety of issues to arise.

Drug Smuggling

Cocaine plays a major role in the modern world. In some South American countries, such as Colombia, cocaine has been so influential that it has largely decided the course of history for the past fifty years.

Colombia is believed to be responsible for two-thirds of the world's coca leaf production and about 80 percent of the world's cocaine manufacturing. A complex network of gangs who produce, smuggle, and supply cocaine (known as "cartels" and led by "drug lords") has arisen in Colombia and some of the surrounding South American countries. The cartels are often exceedingly wealthy and have the ability to fund entire armies to control and protect their interests in land, politics, and smuggling.

The majority of cocaine produced in South America is smuggled into the United States; smaller amounts go to Europe, Australia, and other locations throughout the world. Of the total amount of cocaine seized from 1997 to 1998, 83 percent was seized in the United States and 11 percent in Europe.

Because cocaine smuggling is so profitable, drug cartels will do anything to further their business, often at the high price of civilian losses. Again, the dangers are most severe in Colombia, where fighting between rebels (backed by cocaine interests) and the Colombian government (backed by U.S. dollars) has been ongoing for almost forty years. In the process, an estimated 30,000 people have been killed.

Colombia is *rife* with horror stories surrounding cocaine trafficking. In 1976, for example, Pablo Escobar's arrest for selling cocaine led to a string of deaths. Escobar belonged to the powerful Medellin cartel; soon after his arrest, the police officers who had apprehended him were

Cocaine smuggling is the cause of violence and crime.

Drug cartels affect the economy of Colombia, as well as other South American nations.

assassinated. Next, one judge after another declined to hear the case until all records of the crime mysteriously disappeared.

Colombia's corruption and violence followed cocaine across Florida's borders into the United States. By 1980, Florida's illegal drug trade had become a seven billion–dollar business, outstripping Florida's next largest industry, tourism, by five billion; this terrifying achievement was accomplished by way of the Colombian drug traffickers' violent methods.

Today, Colombian drug cartels control much of the worldwide traffic in illegal substances. In 1989, the U.S. Senate Subcommittee on Terrorism, Narcotic, and International Relations warned that these Colombian cartels are particularly violent. They come from a nation with a history of savage warfare, and Colombian cocaine dealers bring the same style of violence to the cities and neighborhoods they infect around the world.

The massacres committed by Colombian drug dealers often extend to family, friends, and even pets associated with the victims. Savage and gruesome acts are intended to terrify rival dealers. Law enforcement officials who try to resist these drug criminals are sometimes given a choice between "silver or lead," meaning bribes or bullets. Dealers make phone threats, mentioning the names of parents, children, or wives to the individuals they are intimidating. A severed cow tongue might be delivered to the person's home, or strong men may follow the victim throughout the day. Rivals and their families and friends are often murdered.

Even though many of the top Colombian drug traffickers have been taken into police custody, such arrests sometimes merely mean that other competing drug groups have gotten the upper hand. In addition, drug lords have been known to conduct illegal enterprises from behind bars. *The Economist* published an article claiming that Cali cartel leaders in Colombia "have been running their drug business from the comfort of their prison cells." The article describes brutal murders within the prison and speculates that rival drug dealers were responsible for the killings.

For example, on November 5, 1999, a well-dressed man posing as a lawyer strolled into the Palmira maximum-security prison near Cali. He warmly embraced Helmer "Pacho" Herrera—a top dog in the Cali mob—and, in front of other prisoners, shot him six times in the head. Eight days later, Orlando Henao Montoya—the head of the Valle cartel, Cali's one-time ally—was gunned down in another maximum-security prison. This time, it was Pacho's paraplegic brother who fired the shots from his electric wheelchair.

In Colombia itself, the home of these violent groups, this sort of violence is all too common. In one year, seventeen police officers, four judges, and many businesspeople were murdered, while eleven other judges received death threats. At one point, 180 frightened magistrates and judges resigned at once. Democracy and the rule of law withered in the face of such violence. The Colombian government needs outside help to combat the terrifying conditions within their borders.

For the past several years, the United States, Colombia, and Peru have targeted drug-laden aircraft flying between coca-growing regions of Peru and processing laboratories in Colombia. At the same time, a project has been put into effect that provides financial alternatives to coca farmers; these **subsistence farmers** are paid to

The United States has helped fund a program that pays coca farmers to grow other crops.

grow other produce that would otherwise be less lucrative than drug crops. As a result of these two campaigns, coca cultivation in Peru—once the source of more than half the world's cocaine—has decreased 40 percent since the beginning of the project.

The United States also funded the same sort of alternative crop programs in Bolivia as it did in Peru, and these reinforced the Bolivians' own coca-control efforts in the Chapare region. Potential cocaine production declined 13 percent in Bolivia as a result. The amount of land devoted to legal crops in the Chapare is now 127 percent greater than it was in 1986.

Unfortunately, progress in Bolivia and Peru over the past years has been offset by a 56 percent expansion of coca farming in Colombia. Guerrilla and paramilitary forces control these areas where coca is grown. The United States has tried to control the cocaine problem on an agricultural level by paying Colombian pilots to spray poison from the air on coca plants. Almost 99,000 acres of coca were destroyed in this way. The United States increased the amount of money donated to Colombia for fighting illegal drugs from $22 million to $100 million. Because of these efforts, Colombian authorities have been able to arrest seven of their top drug traffickers.

The United States plans to expand their support of the Columbian attack against drug growing. Americans will help police Columbia's rivers and ports, while at the same time working to strengthen alternate crop development programs. The Unites States will also provide training and equipment to judicial systems, law enforcement agencies, and security forces. Meanwhile, America is encouraging the Colombians to cooperate with all these efforts. But the problem still continues.

The United States pays Colombian pilots to spray poison on coca fields.

Prejudice and racial bias play a part in how we imagine drug users; most American drug users are white.

And drug cartels don't only harm drug addicts; they also harm countless individuals throughout the entire supply chain—people who interact with cocaine long before it hits the streets of North America. The people in this chain who are particularly vulnerable are called "mules." Often poor and desperate, these people are recruited or forced by cartels to smuggle cocaine into North America and Europe. The treatment they receive is inhumane, and the dangers they face (bodily harm, death, and almost always imprisonment) are severe, but mules disregard both for the money offered by drug cartels.

Women are often used as mules. Many of these women report trafficking drugs with the intention to support a suffering family; they were lured by drug bosses who offered them sums as large as 2,600 dollars per trip for smuggling cocaine. These women are often forced to swallow packages of more than a pound of cocaine, wrapped in a latex glove or condom; at any moment these packages may break inside the women's stomach or intestines, releasing enormous amounts of cocaine into the carrier's system, causing a quick death. Even so, many women in dire financial situations see no other alternatives and are willing to take the risk.

Crack and Racial Issues

Close your eyes. Now imagine a drug user. What does that person look like? When this question was part of a survey (the results of which were published in the *Journal of Alcohol and Drug Education*), 95 percent of the people who responded pictured someone black; only 5 percent imagined a person from another racial group. The truth is, however, most drug users in the United States are white.

And yet American drug enforcement policies have affected more African Americans than any other group.

An African American man who uses drugs is more likely to be arrested than a white man who uses the same drugs. The African American is more likely to be convicted—and once convicted, he is more apt to receive a more severe sentence. African Americans make up only 13 percent of America's drug users, but 35 percent of all people arrested for drug possession, 55 percent of drug possession convictions, and 74 percent of those sentenced to prison for drug possession are African Americans.

These percentages are the result of three overlapping trends:

1. Drug law enforcement is concentrated in the inner city, where more African Americans live.
2. African Americans who live in inner city areas have fewer treatment programs available to them; as a result, drug abuse in these communities is more likely to be seen as criminal justice problem rather than as a social problem that needs intervention.
3. **Mandatory** sentencing laws are harsher on crack cocaine than powder cocaine. (Crack is cheaper and used by more African Americans than powder cocaine.)

This last policy in regards to crack is the source of one of the biggest controversies surrounding crack and cocaine. In 1986, federal laws created a 100-to-1 ratio between the amount of crack and powder cocaine needed to trigger mandatory sentences. In other words, an offender would receive a five-year sentence for the possession of 500 grams or more of powder cocaine, while

A white man who is arrested for possession of drugs is likely to face a milder sentence than if he were black.

Cocaine—The Rush to Destruction 87

When people are arrested for possession of crack, they are likely to face stiffer sentences than if they were arrested for possession of powder cocaine. Many people believe these differences are actually based on racial prejudice.

another offender would receive the same sentence for only 5 grams of crack. This meant that a dealer who was charged with selling 400 grams of powder cocaine (worth about $40,000) would receive a shorter sentence than the user to whom the dealer sold $500 of crack. Crack was also the only drug that carried a mandatory prison sentence for first-offense possession. Many people felt strongly both for and against these laws.

Those who wanted more severe punishments for crack-related crimes denied that their opinion had anything to do with race. Instead, they listed several other reasons why possessing this form of cocaine was a more serious offense than possessing powder cocaine. For example, they noted that crack is more psychologically addictive, because it produces a quicker and more intense "high" than powder cocaine. The effects of crack also do not last as long as those of powder cocaine, meaning that the user will quickly require more. What's more, crack can be packaged in very small, cheap amounts, while powder cocaine cannot. This means that crack is more likely to be marketed to kids. Crack is usually sold in street markets and "crack houses," which means it makes a definite connection between a particular neighborhood and drug use. This connection leads to the deterioration of that community. In the end, insist those in favor of mandatory sentencing, more violent crime is associated with crack than with powder cocaine.

However, opponents of mandatory harsh sentences for crack possession had their own arguments. They cited the fact that prisons are literally filled with young African Americans serving mandatory sentences for crack crimes. Twenty-one percent of these are classified as "low-level" security risks. (In other words, they have no record of violence, no involvement in more sophisticated criminal activities, and no prior prison experience.) Giving these offenders lighter sentences would save the federal government billions of dollars. Those against mandatory sentencing went on to note that crack and powder cocaine are merely two forms of the same drug, the way beer and whiskey are two forms of alcohol. A person possessing powder cocaine can easily turn it into crack—so why should powder cocaine possession receive a lighter sentence than crack possession? Both forms of the drug are physiologically and psychologically dangerous. People opposed to mandatory sentencing also insisted that violence connected with crack use is actually rare. Alcohol, they pointed out, accounts for far more violent incidents than crack does. And, they added, most of the crime that involves crack is petty theft and prostitution. However, turf wars between Colombian and Cuban drug lords over powder cocaine in the late 1970s and '80s led to thousands of murders.

Is crack use really a more serious offense? Or do law officials perceive crack users to be more dangerous to society simply because these users are often black? The Clinton administration asked Congress to address this possible injustice, and in 1995 the U.S. Sentencing Commission also recommended to Congress that the 100-to-1 ratio be changed. However, Congress eventually rejected the proposal to revise the mandatory sentencing laws. In 1997, the Sentencing Commission again recommended that the difference between crack and powder cocaine sentences be reduced.

Nine years later, in 2006, political arguments continued both for and against harsher mandatory sentences for crack than cocaine. Although many Americans feel the

Although alcohol is far more socially acceptable than cocaine, it is actually responsible for more incidents of violence.

Legal Consequences of Crack

- According to the United States Sentencing Commission, in its 2000 Sourcebook of Federal Sentencing Statistics, the average crack cocaine sentence, 119.5 months, is greater than: the 108-month average sentence for robbery; the 68-month average sentence for arson; the 65-month average sentence for sexual abuse; and the 25-month average sentence for manslaughter.

- Sentences for crack offenders are roughly two to six times as great as sentences for powder cocaine offenders distributing equivalent quantities of drugs.

- Under current federal law, someone caught with five grams of crack cocaine gets a certain five-year sentence—while someone would have to be in possession of 500 grams of the white, powdered cocaine to trigger the same mandatory prison time.

- While a majority of crack users in the United States are white, 94 percent of those sentenced under the incomparably severe penalties for crack cocaine are black or Hispanic.

current drug laws are racist, many others fear that any reduction in the severity of any drug laws will only lead to more drug use in our society.

There is no simple answer. What do you think?

5 Treatment for Cocaine Addiction

Craig didn't want to admit he was addicted to cocaine. He just liked the way it made him feel.

Whenever Craig used cocaine, it stimulated his central nervous system, which then caused a feeling of excitement, a heightening of his senses, an accelerated heart rate, and a reduced desire for sleep. Craig also felt more self-confident, and he had a greater sense of well-being. He wanted to continue having these feelings—but cocaine is a short-acting drug; the desired effects don't last very long.

Individuals who inhale cocaine often want to use the substance again after only ten to thirty minutes. Even when he first started using cocaine, Craig came down from it quickly. That made him depressed, and he immediately began to think about how he could get more

A person who uses cocaine at high levels may experience a variety of negative mental and physical sensations, including auditory and sensory hallucinations.

cocaine so he could experience the exciting feelings again. Before long, Craig's **tolerance** grew, and the amount of cocaine he initially used was no longer enough to produce the effect he craved. As a result, Craig began to use ever-increasing doses of the drug.

When he first experimented with cocaine, Craig was snorting it, but he progressed quickly to using it in all forms, including injections. By the sixth-month anniversary of his new life with cocaine, he was a **compulsive** user. It seemed like no matter how many hits of cocaine Craig took, it was never enough.

At Craig's level of use, new and frightening symptoms started to occur; for example, he heard unpleasant voices that terrified him. Other times he felt like bugs were crawling on his body. When this happened, his heart would pound so fast he was afraid he was going to have a heart attack. These symptoms are typical of individuals who, like Craig, have been using cocaine in high doses over an extended period of time. Eventually, Craig had a **seizure**, which led to hospitalization. That's when Craig made up his mind to do everything possible to end his addiction.

Craig thought he knew what to expect. After all, he had already experienced withdrawal symptoms many times when he was between doses of cocaine. He'd felt an increased need for sleep—and the anxiety and depression of withdrawal.

One of the major challenges in helping someone overcome an addiction to cocaine is encouraging him to resist the lingering urge to use the substance. Craig was physically and emotionally dependent on cocaine, and despite the negative experiences he sometimes had when using it, he experienced a continuous and extreme craving for

Cocaine withdrawal symptoms include but are not limited to:

- agitation
- depression
- intense craving for the drug
- extreme fatigue
- anxiety
- angry outbursts
- lack of motivation
- nausea/vomiting
- shaking
- irritability
- muscle pain
- disturbed sleep

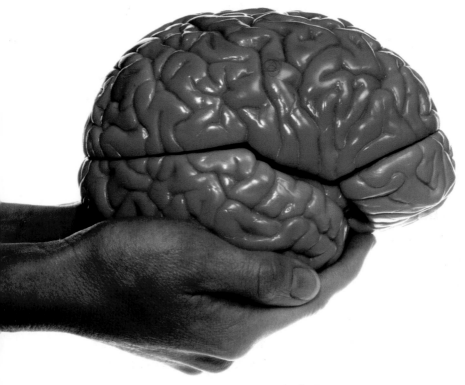

Cocaine causes chemical disruption in the brain.

the substance. One cause of this craving was the fact that cocaine increases dopamine activity in the brain. Along with dopamine, cocaine also keeps both noradrenaline and serotonin active in the brain. These chemicals are responsible for heightened experiences of pleasure.

Remember that when you become addicted to a substance, you interfere with the brain's natural chemical activities. The brain gets used to the chemicals that are introduced into it, and eventually, it and the body builds a tolerance to the substance. As tolerance develops, drug users find they must take more and more of the substance to get the same high they are used to. Trying to eliminate the substance after the brain has built a tolerance to it causes yet more chemical disruption in the brain. Craig interfered with the natural chemical activity in his brain when he began using cocaine, and later, when he tried to discontinue use of cocaine, he altered his brain chemistry yet again. That's when withdrawal symptoms began to occur in his body.

Craig wasn't sure he could stick with his decision to break his addiction on his own. He realized he needed help.

The number of people seeking treatment for cocaine addiction has increased enormously in the past twenty-five years. Today, treatment providers report that cocaine is their clients' most commonly cited drug of abuse. The majority of individuals seeking treatment smoke crack and are likely to be multiple-drug users. Cocaine's widespread abuse has led to extensive efforts to develop treatment programs for this type of drug abuse.

Cocaine abuse and addiction is a complex problem that involves biological changes in the brain. Numerous

Beautiful and Hooked?

Kate Moss is a supermodel and fashion icon. Now, thanks to a stint in drug rehab and a subsequent photo on the cover of a London, England, tabloid in 2005, it seems as though she is—or at least has been—a cocaine user.

Many think of modeling as a glamorous profession—wearing great clothes, traveling all over the world, going to all the hottest parties, and meeting some of the world's most famous people. But, it can be hard work, especially when it comes to maintaining the waiflike appearance for which Kate Moss is known.

It has long been suspected that models use drugs to help them keep that super-thin figure. For most, it's stay thin or lose the modeling gig. Unable to do so on their own, some models have resorted to using drugs, including cocaine and heroin; just a few years ago, heroin-chic was all the rage on high fashion runways.

As for Kate Moss, no one outside of her and her associates know for sure how extensive her drug use has been, or if it continues. She lost some big endorsement and modeling contracts. She issued an apology for the embarrassment she had caused, but did not admit to drug use. Ironically, she now earns more than she did before the scandal hit.

social, family, and environmental factors also come into play. As a result, treating cocaine addiction is a complex process, and it must address a variety of problems.

Behavioral Interventions

Put simply, behavioral treatment programs teach people with addictions to change their behaviors so they are less likely to repeat those that led to addiction in the first place. Unfortunately, nothing about addiction is simple. Though behavioral treatment programs do help those with addictions find ways to avoid behaviors that can cause a relapse, these programs also need to help them discover what led to those behaviors initially.

Supermodel Kate Moss may have used cocaine to help her maintain her thin figure—but despite the rumors, Moss has never admitted to using cocaine.

Cognitive-behavioral therapy helps drug users identify the thought patterns that contribute to their addiction.

Behavioral treatment programs often begin with a period of inpatient treatment. Depending on the length, severity, and drug of addiction, inpatient treatment can be short-term (usually a minimum of thirty days) or long-term residential. At first, some programs allow inpatients to have minimal—if any—contact with the "outside world"; inpatients concentrate on learning about themselves and their relationship with the drug. Later, family and perhaps close friends are encouraged to participate in the treatment program.

Many behavioral treatments have been found to be effective for cocaine addiction, including both residential and outpatient approaches. Behavioral therapies are often the only available, effective treatment approaches to many drug problems, including cocaine addiction.

After stabilization, treatment can take place in an inpatient or outpatient program. Recovery begins with a learning process of breaking old habits and ties with cocaine-using friends, and then identifying the "triggers" that increase the desire to use cocaine.

Cognitive-Behavioral Therapy

A cognitive-behavioral approach to treatment encourages users to identify thought patterns and habits that have contributed to their habits. This is a short-term, focused approach to helping cocaine-addicted individuals become abstinent from cocaine and other substances. The underlying assumption is that learning processes play an important role in the development and continuation of cocaine abuse and dependence.

The same learning processes can be used to help individuals reduce drug use. This approach attempts to help patients to recognize the situations in which they are

In his book *Recovery Options: The Complete Guide*, Joseph Volpicelli, M.D., Ph.D., lists six stages of change that define the process of recovery from use of addictive substances, and points out that an individual rarely moves through them (from precontemplation to termination) in a linear manner. According to Dr. Volpicelli, people with a substance-related disorder are much more likely to move through the stages in a cyclical manner until they achieve termination.

- Precontemplation: Giving up the substance has not yet been contemplated.
- Contemplation: The individual is thinking about the situation and deciding if she wants to stop her dependence on the substance.
- Preparation: The person is getting ready to take action.
- Action: The individual is actively engaged in discontinuing substance use.
- Maintenance: Efforts are exerted to sustain remission.
- Termination: A maintenance program is no longer needed.

most likely to use cocaine, avoid these situations when appropriate, and cope more effectively with a range of problems and behaviors associated with drug abuse.

Patients are encouraged to specifically identify these triggers and to restructure their lifestyles to avoid them. Many patients identify certain music or movies with cocaine and must learn to deal with these issues. An old Chinese proverb speaks to the issue of craving cocaine and relapse: "You can't help it if a bird lands on your head. But you don't have to let him build a nest." In other words, if a person entertains the thought of cocaine long enough, it gains the power to impair her judgment and influence her behavior. Cocaine abusers become experts at self-deception, creating reasons to use more cocaine; this therapy seeks to break through the lies.

Counseling on Spiritual and Emotional Issues

Perhaps the most difficult aspect of treatment and recovery from cocaine involves the guilt and intense shame felt by most users. Addiction can cause individuals to act in ways contrary to their previous values and morals. Acknowledging their actions can be extremely difficult, so difficult, in fact, that the guilt associated with these behaviors becomes a major reason to use still more cocaine. Getting high is, in a sense, a short vacation from the intense guilt and shame associated with cocaine addiction.

Finding spiritual strength through religious practices can help individuals with an addiction.

Dealing with these painful issues takes time and trust. An experienced counselor, another recovering addict, or a trusted clergy person can offer help. Most good treatment programs have these people on staff.

Residential Programs

Therapeutic communities, or residential programs with planned lengths of stay of six to twelve months, offer another alternative to those in need of treatment for cocaine addiction. Therapeutic communities are often comprehensive; they focus on the resocialization of the individual to society, and can include on-site *vocational rehabilitation* and other supportive services. Therapeutic communities typically are used to treat patients with more severe problems, such as *co-occurring* mental health problems and criminal involvement.

Self-Help Programs

Twelve-step programs offer support by helping cocaine abusers accept their problems by learning from other recovering addicts that there is life after cocaine. These programs include:

- Cocaine Anonymous (CA)
- Narcotics Anonymous (NA)
- Alcoholics Anonymous (AA)

Based on the twelve-step program of Alcoholics Anonymous (AA), Narcotics Anonymous (NA) and Cocaine Anonymous help those addicted to drugs such as cocaine stay sober in the outside world. The first NA

The Twelve Steps

1. We admitted we were powerless over drugs—that our lives had become unmanageable.

2. Came to believe that a Power greater than ourselves could restore us to sanity.

3. Made a decision to turn our will and our lives over to the care of God as we understand Him.

4. Made a searching and fearless moral inventory of ourselves.

5. Admitted to God, and to our selves, and to another human being the exact nature of our wrongs.

6. We're entirely ready to have God remove all these defects of character.

7. Humbly asked Him to remove our shortcomings.

8. Made a list of all persons we had harmed, and became willing to make amends to them all.

9. Made direct amends to such people wherever possible, except when to do so would injure them or others.

10. Continued to take personal inventory and when we were wrong promptly admitted it.

11. Sought through prayer and meditation to improve our conscious contact with God as we understand Him, praying only for knowledge of His will for us and the power to carry that out.

12. Having had a spiritual awakening as the result of these steps, we tried to carry this message to drug addicts and to practice these principles in all our affairs.

Rehabilitation or "rehab" programs traditionally have the following basic elements:

- initial evaluation
- abstinence
- learning about addiction
- group counseling
- AA or other twelve-step participation
- individual counseling
- a family program

meetings were held in the early 1950s in Los Angeles, California. As found on its Web site (www.na.org), the organization described itself this way in its first publication:

> NA is a nonprofit fellowship or society of men and women for whom drugs had become a major problem. We . . . meet regularly to help each other stay clean. . . . We are not interested in what or how much you used . . . but only in what you want to do about your problem and how we can help.

In the more than fifty years since, NA has grown into one of the largest organizations of its kind. Today, groups are located all over the world, and its books and pamphlets are published in thirty-two languages. No matter where the group is located, each chapter is based on the twelve steps first formulated in AA, which emphasize taking responsibility for behavior, making amends to others, and self-forgiveness. Successful recovery programs strongly urge daily attendance at twelve-step meetings for the first

The Twelve Steps encourages those with an addiction to take personal inventory while using prayer and meditation to seek a relationship with a "Higher Power."

If you are addicted to cocaine, there is no pill you can take to treat your condition, but researchers are looking for pharmacological approaches to this addiction.

Chapter 5—Treatment for Cocaine Addiction

ninety days of sobriety. Individuals who successfully abstain from cocaine attend a lot of twelve-step meetings for support and accountability. They often report that a part of them still looks for a good reason to use cocaine—but twelve-step meetings, such as those associated with CA and NA, give them daily reminders of their powerlessness over drugs.

Pharmacological Approaches

Successful treatment of many addictions is often enhanced by the use of carefully prescribed medications. However, there are currently no medications available to specifically treat cocaine addiction. Consequently, the National Institute of Drug Abuse (NIDA) is aggressively pursuing the identification and testing of new cocaine treatment medications. Attempts are even being made to develop a vaccine to cocaine, so that cocaine users could conceivably be made immune to its effects.

Several newly emerging compounds are being investigated to assess their safety and *efficacy* in treating cocaine addiction. Because of mood changes experienced during the early stages of cocaine abstinence, antidepressant drugs have shown some benefit. In addition to the problems of treating addiction, cocaine overdose results in many deaths every year, and medical treatments are being developed to deal with the acute emergencies resulting from excessive cocaine abuse.

Addiction to cocaine is a physical disease. A person addicted to cocaine may do "bad" things and commit crimes to support his habit—but this does not mean that the person himself is evil. Instead, he suffers from a physiological

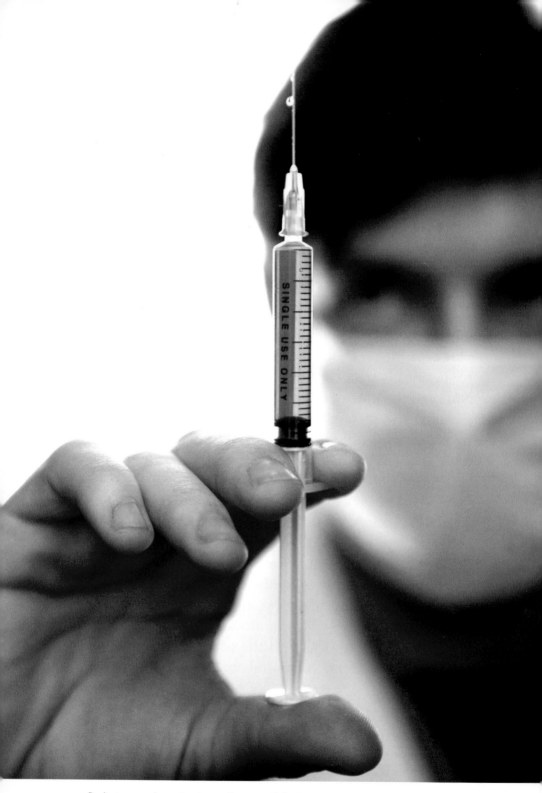

Perhaps one day, scientists will successfully develop a vaccine that will make cocaine users immune to the drug's effects.

condition, one that is very difficult to treat. Treatment can be successful, however. Around the world, the medical and legal communities are working together to find answers to the cocaine problem.

High school students may turn to marijuana as a way to be more comfortable socially; marijuana use can sometimes escalate to "harder" drugs such as cocaine.

The path to sobriety is not an easy one, especially if the individual is addicted to more than one substance. Josh tells his story on the Partnership for a Drug-Free American Web site (www.drugfree.org):

My life started out like many others. I was born in Madison, Wisconsin, and raised in a middle-class family. My father was in the Marine Corps, so we moved around a few times but I had a fun childhood and a loving and caring family who would do anything for me.

When I got to high school things changed. I felt distant from people, and had to fight harder to have friends—and I was shy all the time. Then I began hanging out with older kids, going to parties and skipping school. My parents didn't like my new friends and enforced strict rules.

I quit school and my relationship with my family fell apart. I started smoking pot and drinking heavily. I was taking Mushrooms and acid daily. Finally, I wasn't shy around people anymore. I had more "friends" than ever before and for the first time I felt like I was a part of something. People wanted to hang out with me. I felt cool.

But I couldn't hold a job for more than three months. Sometimes when I needed money, I would steal my parents' mortgage money and other savings they had stashed away.

My parents made me do random drug testing to prove that I was sober. To get around this I found someone who didn't use and carried her urine around with me in case I was tested.

I started dating a girl who introduced me to Cocaine. The first time I tried it I felt great—very social and unafraid of anything. It started out as a weekend thing. Eventually I was using so much I began selling it.

I lost weight and started having bloody noses. My parents became suspicious. They questioned me but I always denied everything. Eventually they had our phones tapped and heard me buying drugs and selling drugs. One night I came home from a six-day binge and they questioned me again. Still I denied it. So they pulled out the tape recorder. Busted!

My parents urged me to go to rehab but I refused. They threatened to kick me out if I didn't do something, so I agreed to quit doing drugs. But after two weeks I gave in.

I started drinking again and quickly fell back into my old habits. I left my parents house and went to live with a friend. For the next three years I was drinking, smoking and doing coke—and selling drugs to support my habit. I was out of control. I had to use just to feel okay. Wherever I went anywhere I had to first get high.

I was staying at different people's houses. Eventually I gave up my cocaine addiction for pills. I figured if I ate pills instead of snorting cocaine I was doing all right. WRONG! My pill addiction grew worse than ever. Everyday for the next two years I used morphine, methadone, Percocet, Vicodin, Ultram, Oxy-Contin, Xanax or just about anything I could get my hands on. I kept telling myself as long as I'm not using coke I'm okay.

One night I couldn't find anything—no pills, no pot, I even looked for coke. Eventually, I stumbled across Heroin and snorted it. Some people told me that the high was a million times better if you shot it. So I did. Two seconds after pushing the heroin into my veins I felt like God. Nothing in the whole world compared to this experience. I fell in love.

I shot heroin for almost six months. I was friends with the dealer so it was easy to get. Then my dealer got busted. I didn't know what to do. I went to the hospital and told them I was detoxing from heroin. They took me in for a few hours and gave me something called a Clonidine patch, which worked great for a few days.

When I woke up on the seventh day I felt horrible. I could only think about where I could get something, anything. No one had any drugs. So I started drinking so heavily that I'm lucky I'm alive today to talk about it. I was stealing beer and borrowing money almost everyday. Eventually the drugs came back around and I felt okay again.

I met a girl through work and we started dating. She partied just as much as I did. We would go out and party together, using, selling and doing whatever would get us high—including coke. Things seemed pretty good for a few months. I stopped using heroin and cocaine and I slowed down on Alcohol. I still ate pills everyday but at least I wasn't using the heavier drugs.

Then my girlfriend started feeling nauseous and we found out that she was pregnant. This changed everything for us. We decided that we wanted to keep the baby. We made an agreement to each other to stop using everything: cigarettes, alcohol and all drugs. I thought it would be easy because now I had a real reason to get my life back together. I was wrong—it wasn't any easier for me to quit this time than any other time before.

My girlfriend was able to quit but I couldn't. So, I lied to her and secretly continued to take pills. I was hardly making enough money to sustain us and I was selling drugs on the side to support my habit that no one knew about.

At 6 a.m. December 17th, 2002, the Drug Task Force team knocked on my door with a warrant for my arrest. My girlfriend, who was six-months pregnant, and I were both charged with the sales of narcotics and spent the night in jail. The next morning our parents got us out—her bail was $500 and mine was $5,000.

At this point I was scared and had no drugs. But I was ready to get some real help—I admitted myself to a four-month intensive inpatient stay.

In the beginning I fought the program. I was scared and hated being away from my girlfriend. I was also coming off of some heavy drugs. During the halfway point of the program, they held a family weekend. My family expressed how my drug use had affected them. I saw what I'd put them through all those years. I also learned about my girlfriend's nervousness and distrust and how mad she was at me for lying about the drugs. My parents said this was the last straw—if I didn't stop after this they would basically disown me, and my girlfriend said she would take our child and leave me no matter how hard that would be for her.

Basically, I realized that I was hurting the people that loved me the most. I didn't want to lose them. I decided to give sobriety a hundred percent. I wanted people to know me for ME, not as a drug addict. It was a very emotional weekend for everyone. After the visit I was more accepting of the program and I successfully completed it on March 25.

I returned home three weeks before the birth of my beautiful baby girl, Deja Kai, on April 13. I was so excited to be able to be there. My girlfriend and I had gotten married two weeks earlier.

Today I struggle with my sobriety. I attend a weekly outpatient program, go to meetings almost every day and to family counseling with my wife. I'm learning to live a whole new life than what I've been used. I never knew how sucked in I was until I got sober. I feel like drugs will always be a part of me. I have to work hard every day of my life.

Because of my addiction and the sales of narcotics I've been charged with six felony counts of sales. This has caused more stress and anxiety than I've ever experienced. My state does not have drug courts yet so the state is trying to sentence me to go to state prison for several years. I'm currently fighting these charges because if I weren't using drugs I would never have sold them.

Now I'm 26 years old, married and have a beautiful daughter. I work about 30 hours a week in my father's construction company. I've been sober for 12 months—it's the first time in almost 13 years. I'm currently taking medication for depression and anxiety, obsessive-compulsive disorder, and a drug called Naltrexone that blocks the opiate receptors so I don't feel the craving for narcotics.

Life is completely different being sober. I now wake up each morning and can get to work on time. I have extra money to pay my bills and do activities with my family. I'm writing music for a new band that I'm in called Side Project. I feel great! It feels rewarding to be clean, sober and focused. In a weird way, getting arrested was the best thing that could have ever happened to me—because I got sober!

Since my sobriety I want to help as many people as I can who struggle with drug addiction. I feel that I owe it to people who suffer from this disease. If I can find true happiness in my sobriety than I believe that everyone who suffers from this disease, deserves to find true happiness in their lives as well.

Rehab programs help users find practical ways to overcome their addictions.

Chapter 5—Treatment for Cocaine Addiction

What Do Rehab Programs Accomplish?

Abstinence

In many cases it seems that as long as the substance is in the blood stream, thinking remains distorted. Often during the first days or weeks of total abstinence, we see a gradual clearing of thinking processes. This is a complex psychological and biological phenomenon, and is one of the elements that inpatient programs are able to provide by making sure the patient is fully detoxified and remains abstinent during his or her stay.

Removal of Denial

In some cases, when someone other than the patient, such as a parent, employer, or other authority, is convinced there is a problem, but the addict is not yet sure, voluntary attendance at a rehab program will provide enough clarification to remove this basic denial. Even those who are convinced they have a problem with substances usually don't admit to themselves or others the full extent of the addiction. Rehab uses group process to identify and help the individual to let go of these expectable forms of denial.

Removal of Isolation

As addictions progress, relationships deteriorate in quality. However, the bonds between fellow recovering people are widely recognized as one of the few forces powerful enough to keep recovery on track. The rehab experience, whether it is inpatient or outpatient involves in-depth sharing in a group setting. This kind of sharing creates strong interpersonal bonds among group members. These bonds help to form a support system that will be powerful enough to sustain the individual during the first months of abstinence.

"Basic Training"

Basic training is a good way to think of the experience of rehab. Soldiers need a rapid course to give them the basic knowledge and skills they will need to fight in a war. Some kinds of learning need to be practiced so well that you can do them without thinking. In addition to the learning, trainees become physically fit, and perhaps most important, form emotional bonds that help keep up morale when the going is hard.

(*Source*: Partnership for a Drug-Free America.)

Glossary

amphetamines: Drugs that stimulant the central nervous system, used to treat conditions such as depression and as an appetite suppressant.

base: A chemical compound having a pH value between 8 and 14 that reacts with acids to form salts.

black market: A system of illegally buying and selling officially controlled goods.

compulsive: Driven by an irresistible inner force to do something.

contracted: Caught an illness.

co-occurring: Happening at the same time.

demographic: Relating to the characteristics of the human population.

efficacy: The ability to produce the desired result.

hormone: A regulatory chemical in the body.

idolatry: Extreme admiration or fanatical devotion to someone or something.

infectious: Able to cause illness via the spread of micro-organisms.

Kaposi's sarcoma: A form of cancer found predominately in people with weakened immune systems.

lymphoma: A tumor that forms in a lymph node.

mandatory: Required.

melancholy: Sadness.

neurotransmitter: A chemical that aids in the transmission of messages in the body.

opportunistic: Taking advantage of a situation.

oxidation: A chemical reaction in which oxygen is added to an element or compound.

pathogen: Something that can cause a disease.

pneumocystis carinii pneumonia: A form of pneumonia often found in people with weakened immune systems.

Quechua: A member of any of several native South America peoples, including the Incas, living in the Andes.

rife: Widespread.

sanctions: Penalties for breaking a law or rule.

seizure: The physical manifestations (as convulsions, sensory disturbances, or loss of consciousness) resulting from abnormal electrical discharges in the brain (as in epilepsy).

stable: Not subject to changes in chemical or physical properties.

subsistence farmers: Farmers that produce only enough to provide for their families, with little or nothing left over to sell.

tolerance: The loss of a normal response to a drug because of repeated exposure to it.

toxoplasmosis: A disease in mammals that is transmitted to humans through undercooked meat or through contact with infected animals, especially cats.

tuberculosis: A highly contagious lung disease.

vasoconstriction: The narrowing of blood vessels resulting in the reduction of blood flow or increased blood pressure.

vocational rehabilitation: Rehabilitation designed to provide the needed skills for a particular job or career.

Further Reading

Apel, Melanie Ann. *Cocaine and Your Nose: The Incredibly Disgusting Story*. New York: Rosen, 2000.

Carlson-Berne, Emma (ed.). *Cocaine*. Farmington Hills, Mich.: Thomson Gale, 2005.

Carroll, Marilyn. *Cocaine and Crack*. Berkeley Heights, N.J.: Enslow, 2001.

Landau, Elaine. *Cocaine*. New York: Scholastic Library, 2003.

Lennard-Brown, Sarah. *Cocaine*. Chicago, Ill.: Raintree, 2005.

Peck, Rodney G. *Crack*. New York: Rosen, 2000.

Robbins, Paul R. *Crack and Cocaine Drug Dangers*. Berkeley Heights, N.J.: Enslow, 2001.

For More Information

Cocaine Anonymous (CA)
www.ca.org

Drugs: What You Should Know
www.kidshealth.org/PageManager.jsp?dn=familydoctor&lic=44&article_set=22660

Narcotics Anonymous (NA)
www.na.org

NIDA for Teens: Facts on Drugs—Stimulants
teens.drugabuse.gov/facts/facts_stiml.asp

Partnership for a Drug-Free America
drugfree.org

Teen Drug Abuse
www.teendrugabuse.us

Teen Drug Abuse and Addiction—Cocaine Facts
www.teen-drug-abuse.org.hard-facts-about-cocaine.htm

The Web sites listed on this page were active at the time of publication. The publisher is not responsible for Web sites that have changed their addresses or discontinued operation since the date of publication. The publisher will review and update the Web-site list upon each reprint.

Bibliography

American Heart Association. "Tobacco Industry's Targeting of American Psychiatric Association. "Cocaine and Related Disorders." http://www.minddisorders.com/Br-Del/Cocaine-and-related-disorders.html.

"Crack Cocaine." http://www.cocaine.org.

Grinspoon, Lester, and James Bakalar. *Cocaine: A Drug and Its Social Evolution*. New York: Basic Books, 1976.

"History of Cocaine and Crack Use." http://www.intheknowzone.com/cocaine/history.htm.

National Institutes of Health. "Cocaine Abuse and Addiction." http://www.nida.nih.gov.

Index

Picture Credits

Author and Consultant Biographies

Author

Zachary Chastain is a poetry editor currently living in Chicago, Illinois, where he is also continuing his education in English and communications. He has published numerous short stories and poems. This is his first book for Mason Crest.

Series Consultant

Jack E. Henningfield, Ph.D., is a professor at the Johns Hopkins University School of Medicine, and he is also Vice President for Research and Health Policy at Pinney Associates, a consulting firm in Bethesda, Maryland, that specializes in science policy and regulatory issues concerning public health, medications development, and behavior-focused disease management. Dr. Henningfield has contributed information relating to addiction to numerous reports of the U.S. Surgeon General, the National Academy of Sciences, and the World Health Organization.